Little green BOOKS™

Santa Claus Is Green!
How to Have an Eco-Friendly Christmas

By Alison Inches
Illustrated by Wednesday Kirwan

LITTLE SIMON • An imprint of Simon & Schuster Children's Publishing Division • New York London Toronto Sydney • 1230 Avenue of the Americas, New York, New York 10020 • Copyright © 2009 by Simon & Schuster, Inc. • Book design by Laura Reddick • All rights reserved, including the right of reproduction in whole or in part in any form. LITTLE SIMON is a registered trademark of Simon & Schuster, Inc., and associated colophon is a trademark of Simon & Schuster, Inc. • LITTLE GREEN BOOKS and associated colophon are trademarks of Simon & Schuster, Inc. • For information about special discounts for bulk purchases, please contact Simon & Schuster Special Sales at 1-866-506-1949 or business@simonandschuster.com. The Simon & Schuster Speakers Bureau can bring authors to your live event. For more information or to book an event contact the Simon & Schuster Speakers Bureau at 1-866-248-3049 or visit our website at www.simonspeakers.com. Manufactured in the United States of America 0909 LAK • First Edition • 10 9 8 7 6 5 4 3 2 1 • ISBN 978-1-4169-7223-5

The day after Christmas, Santa received an important letter.

Dear Santa,

Christmas is not good for the Earth! I went outside with my brand-new remote-control car, but there was nowhere to play. Trash bags were tumbling down the street, wrapping paper was popping the lids right off the trash cans, and the curbs were already lined with Christmas tree skeletons! You have to help!

Your friend,
Billy

P.S. Did you know that most of the paper in the world is used to make packages?

P.P.S. No need to box or wrap my presents next year!

Santa wasn't feeling jolly after he read Billy's letter. "The Earth is so beautiful," said Santa. "The last thing I want to do is spoil it."

So Santa thought and thought until . . .

"I know!" said Santa, filling with new holiday cheer.
"This year I'll give a gift to the Earth!"

Santa began to dream of a green Christmas. He made a list—and checked it twice. He had to make sure it was Earth-friendly and nice.

Packaging Reduction

Green Santa Fact:
Between November and December, we throw away an extra one million tons of trash per week. That's the same weight as 200,000 full-grown elephants!

"This year I won't waste a thing," Santa declared.

The elves loved the idea of a green Christmas! At Santa's Repair Shop old toys were made new again, and at Santa's Recycled Present Factory brand-new toys were made out of recycled papers, plastics, and metals.

"Good work, my little helpers!" cheered Santa proudly. "Repairing and recycling toys means less waste on Earth."

When it was time to put up the Christmas tree, Santa and Mrs. Claus planted a tree in a beautiful pot. Now they could replant it in the spring.

"We can remember Christmas all year round," said Santa. "And we'll be giving a gift to the Earth!"

Instead of hanging lights or new decorations, Santa and the elves surprised Mrs. Claus by covering the tree with ornaments they made from old Christmas cards.

"This is wonderful!" exclaimed Mrs. Claus. "We'll think of our friends and family each time we look at our tree!"

"Let's decorate the workshop," said Santa. "This year, the North Pole is going to be green!" Aluminum cans became candle holders and bells, milk cartons became Christmas ornaments, and plastic containers became snowmen.

Mrs. Claus baked cookie ornaments and made a gingerbread house while the elves made colorful garlands from popcorn and cranberries. Everything looked good enough to eat!

"Ho, ho, ho! It's so much jollier decorating with things you've made yourself!" said Santa.

Even gift-giving became jollier with green gifts. Santa and Mrs. Claus gave gifts of sparkling cookies, sweet pies, and chocolates that they made together. Their presents were wrapped in colorful newspaper pages, old maps, and shopping bags.

"Homemade gifts are so much sweeter!" said Mrs. Claus with a giggle.

There was a special gift for Santa, too. Mrs. Claus and the elves had made him a bright green suit and hat with fleece made from recycled plastic.

"Green is my new favorite color!" said Santa.

On Christmas Eve . . .

Santa dressed in his new green suit and loaded all of the Earth-friendly gifts into his sleigh.

"For the love of the Earth!" he called out to the
reindeer. "We'll do what we should!
Reducing!
Reusing!
Recycling for good!"

All over the world Santa filled Christmas stockings with dolls made from organic cotton, handmade teddy bears, and homemade treats wrapped in recycled paper.

At every delivery Santa made sure to . . .

turn off the lights to save energy . . .

close the windows to save heat . . .

and eat every last cookie so none would go to waste!

He also left a little guide to help every little boy and girl have a very merry green Christmas and an eco-friendly new year.

On Christmas Day everyone was excited to find Earth-friendly presents that were way more fun than any they'd received before. And knowing they were helping save the Earth made everyone feel good on the inside, too.

Soon everyone wanted to go green like Santa.

When the Christmas celebrations were over, children helped recycle their Christmas trees, and they stored their smoothed-out wrapping paper, ribbons, boxes, and cards for next year.
It was the happiest Christmas on—and for the—Earth!

A few days after Christmas, Santa got another important letter.

Dear Santa,

I love my awesome mountain bike! I can't believe it was made from recycled aluminum! But my favorite gift is the list of tips you left for me. I'm going to ride my bike and find ways to use your ideas to keep our world green.

Keep up the good work, Santa, and we will too!

Your friend,
Billy

Santa sat at his desk and smiled. "If everyone changed one of their wasteful habits every month," said Santa, "every day would be as jolly, green, and bright as this Christmas!"

You can be a green Santa too by trying out Santa's simple suggestions!

Santa's Twelve Ideas for a Green Christmas

1. Walk or ride your bike to the store when you shop, and take a reusable bag.

2. Make homemade presents for friends and family.

3. Remind your mom and dad to cancel any magazines or shopping catalogs they may no longer read.

4. Wrap presents in comics, decorated paper bags, or maps.

5. Clean out your old toys and give them to friends or to a charity.

6. Make gift tags by cutting out the pictures on old Christmas cards.

7. Give the gift of showing someone how to do something—like riding a bike or making a friendship bracelet.

8. Save energy by turning off the TV and playing games like charades or checkers with your family and friends.

9. Pack gifts that need to be mailed in the smallest box possible.

10. E-mail an e-card to your family and friends instead of sending holiday cards.

11. Don't hang lights on your house and tree. Instead, decorate with festive garlands you can make from popcorn, cranberries, dried fruits, and recycled paper.

12. Buy a Christmas tree potted in soil and replant it after the holiday.